This book is for all of the kids who have two houses, and my brothers, Aidan and Finnegan.

www.mascotbooks.com

Two Houses

©2020 Hunter Novak. All Rights Reserved. No part of this publication may be reproduced, stored in a retrieval system or transmitted in any form by any means electronic, mechanical, or photocopying, recording or otherwise without the permission of the author.

For more information, please contact:
Mascot Books
620 Herndon Parkway, Suite 320
Herndon, VA 20170
info@mascotbooks.com

Library of Congress Control Number: 2019910856

CPSIA Code: PRT0919A
ISBN-13: 978-1-64543-072-8

Printed in the United States

TWO HOUSES

Hunter Novak
Illustrated by Juan Diaz

And this is my mom.

When I was three, my mom and dad got a divorce. This means they are not married anymore.

I have one brother at my mommy's house. We have so much fun fishing and crabbing when I'm at her house.

I have one brother at my daddy's house. We love to wrestle and ride four wheelers when I'm there!

Even though I love having two houses, it is not always easy for me.

Sometimes I feel sad. Sometimes I feel angry.

Sometimes I wonder, why can't I be like other kids that have just one house and one mom and dad?

They sit together at my soccer games.

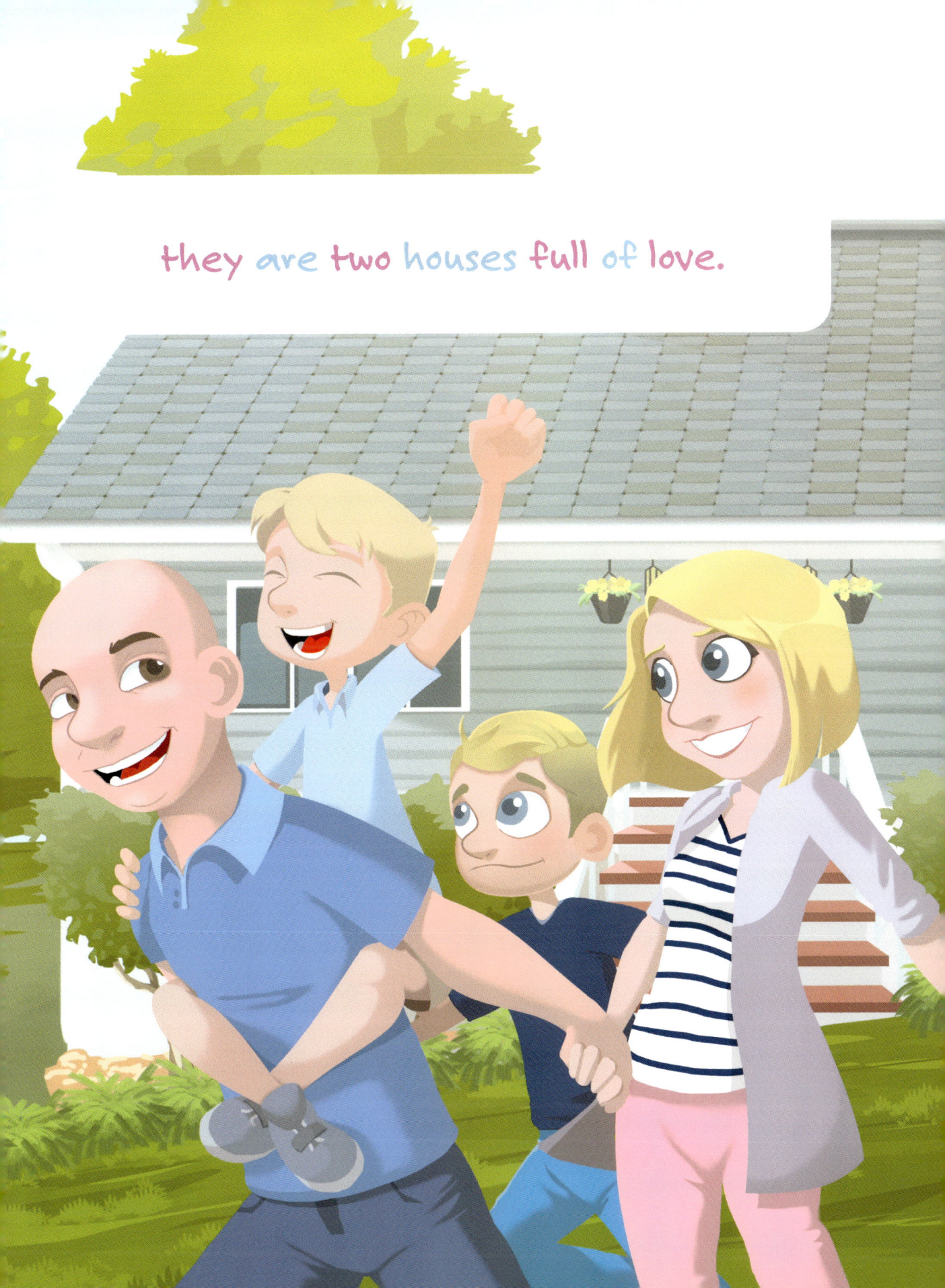

THE END

About the Author

Hunter Novak is a nine-year-old fourth grader from Smithfield, Virginia. His parents have been divorced for six years, and while they get along, it's not always easy for him to go back and forth despite the positives about both homes. Hunter loves to play soccer and excels in math. His favorite thing to do is spend time with his brothers, Aidan and Finnegan.